JACK OF BOTH SIDES

THE STORY OF A SCHOOL WAR

FLORENCE COOMBE

CHAPTER I. THE JOKE THAT FAILED.

"I say, you fellows, look here! What do you think of this? It's our lunch!"

"This" was a large basket, lined with a white cloth, at the bottom of which lay nine bread-pills. Nine boys looked down at them in rueful disgust, and then across the school-room to where a larger group stood chuckling mischievously, their hands and mouths filled with tempting, crusty hunches, carved from the loaf according to fancy.

Those nine gray, unappetizing pellets represented all that was left of the loaf; and Mason, the boy who first spoke, realizing this, flung the big basket in a burst of indignation at the heads of the opposite clump, one or two of whom were hit. Revenge was prompt. Ere it touched the floor it was hurled back with vigour, but, being dodged successfully, fell harmless to the ground.

Mason and seven others were new-comers to Brincliffe School, and when the luncheon interval was heralded by the entrance of the loaf and the exit of the masters, it did not occur to them to join in the general rush that was made at the basket. And this was the sorry reward of good manners!

The fact of the matter is that they were not merely new boys, and therefore lawful game, but day-pupils. That was a grievance at Brincliffe—a great grievance. It was only last term that the first day-boy was admitted into Mr. West's establishment. More than one young wiseacre had gloomily prophesied that Jim Bacon was the thin end of the wedge. And now they gloated, "Didn't we say so?"

It is not easy to see at once what objection there could be to certain boys attending the school and yet sleeping in their own homes. But a rooted objection there undoubtedly was—all the stronger, perhaps, because no valid reason for it could be stated.

Now for a few moments words took the place of missiles.

"You—you greedy, giggling gobblers—you!" This was from Mason, and he was hungry. The "g's" came out in slow, studied jerks.

"And what are you, pray? A pack of pretty poppets! Mammy's darlings! Must go home to by-by, mustn't you?" Sneering was Joe Green's forte.

Words failed Mason, but a small black-eyed lad, called Lewis Simmons, took up the cudgels in his stead.

"I'd rather be a pretty poppet than an ugly chimpanzee like — *some* people!"

"Hold your tongue, baby! Cheek me again, and you'll get smacked. We must see that all you duckies go to bed at twelve for a little nap. You shall have a nice beauty-sleep, you shall!"

"Don't answer! Swallow it down!" muttered Jack Brady, laying his hand on Simmons's shoulder. "Let 'em have the last word if they're stuck on it. We're only wasting breath."

"It's all very well, Brady, but they have treated us abominably! We'd done nothing to them." Ethelbert Hughes, who said this in a low voice, was Simmons's special chum, though a great contrast, being tall and fair, with a gentle, quiet manner.

"Still, there's nothing gained by bandying names," returned Brady. "And it isn't even amusing to listen to. A fellow's seldom funny and furious at the same time.

"I don't care about words," said Mason, giving a fierce kick to the basket. "I'm quite ready to bandy thumps, if they prefer it. But they de serve trouncing in some way for a caddish trick like this."

"It was a bit rough on us, but they only meant it as a joke," persisted Brady. "We must pay them back in joke, and then it'll be all right."

"Will it?" growled Bacon. "I know better. Why, they hate day-boys like poison, and they'll let you all feel it too. I had a nice dose of it last term, and I'm jolly glad there are some more of you to share it with me this time."

"Oh, that's it, is it?" said a boy called Armitage. "And are they all such donkeys as to care whether we sleep here or not?"

"They're all such sheep as to follow the same track blindly, and not dare to act on their own hook," replied Bacon. "It's the fashion to run down day-boys, that's all. But it's a beastly shame, and I almost wish West hadn't let me in."

"Oh, rubbish!" said Brady. "Fashions change quickly. We'll have a ripping time, in spite of everybody."

Meanwhile the boarders were discussing matters from their point of view.

"It's just what I expected," said Norman Hallett, a tall, well-built boy, who was the eldest in the school. "Once open the door—only a chink—and in pours the whole town." He waved a half-eaten crust to illustrate the pouring in.

"West had better drop the name of Brincliffe, and call us Elmridge Grammar School at once. That's what we are now," observed Green.

"I don't mind so much about that," said a grave-faced boy, whose name was Vickers; "but what I do hate is the way day-boys spoil everything. It can't be helped, but nothing's ever fair or equal when once day-boys get mixed up with a school. I'll tell you exactly what happens. First"—and here the speaker laid his forefinger on his thumb to mark the order—"First, they're always trying to make you green with envy by talking about the jolly things they're going to. Second, they're continually getting holidays for themselves on some pretence or other. Third, they love to pity you, and declare they'd shoot themselves rather than be regular boarders. Fourth, they buy cribs and keys, and keep them at home, and get help from their fathers, and work extra hours, and spoil your chance of a prize altogether. Fifth, they're for ever sniggering over private jokes about people you neither know nor want to—"

"Hold, Vickers, my dear chap!" broke in Cadbury, the school jester. "It pains me to check the fluency of our golden-mouthed orator, but I've been waiting in vain for 'Finally'. Let's have an innings. What I object to is that they're such a horrid lot. Cocky to a degree—simply think no end of themselves—and lose their hair altogether at the first little playful joke. I think the beastly way in which they took that bread game spoke for itself. I should like to have hammered them for that."

"West will be changing all our hours and classes soon to suit the convenience of the day-boarders. That'll be the next move. I know it, because I heard him ask that gawky chap they call Mason if he could stay on Wednesday evenings for the dancing class. If he could, indeed! That's the way they're going to be treated."

"If they are, it'll be war to the knife between us and them," observed Hallett, folding his arms with an air of conscious might.

"War wiz knife, Hallett? Ah!"

It was a black-browed foreign child of nine who whispered these words, creeping close to Hallett, and gazing up curiously into his face. Hallett burst out laughing.

"Listen to this bloodthirsty brigand of a March Hare! The instinct of his ancestors is strong within him. No, Harey," he continued, "I won't stickle for knives, or even pistols. Shall we call it war to the fist? Anything will do, so long as it's war."

"What do you all think of the weekly? Is he as bad as the rest?" asked Grey, one of the juniors. He was always careful to find out what he ought to think before he thought it.

"Which is the weakly one?" asked Cadbury. "That lily-flower bending on its stalk to address the cheeky, black-eyed imp? He looks weakly enough, all eyes and hair."

"No, no; that's Hughes, from the Bank. I mean the new weekly boarder, who's to go home from Saturday to Monday."

"I know the one," said Hallett. "The apple-faced boy who does so much laughing. I heard someone call him Brady."

"Oh, that fellow! He doesn't look so bad," pronounced Trevelyan, who ranked only second to Hallett.

"He seems to have a strong sense of humour," remarked Vickers gravely, at which his comrades giggled. Vickers was commonly believed to have none. He never laughed when anyone else did.

"A weekly boarder is a very different thing from a day-boy," Hallett went on. "If Brady was wise he wouldn't go mixing himself up with that lot. I shall give him a wrinkle when he comes my way. He really looks rather decent, and he was the only one who grinned about the bread. Of course it may have been from sheer force of habit, and therefore no credit to him; but still, he did grin."

At this moment the discussion in both camps was brought to a sudden finish by the return of the masters. The chief himself, Mr. West, was the first to enter, and his eye was immediately caught by the bread basket, which lay dejected on its side in a little pool of crumbs. He looked suspiciously at it.

"Who threw the basket on the floor?"

Dead silence.

"Come, speak out! Someone must have done it; baskets don't jump off tables by themselves."

After another short silence, one of the young day-pupils, who happened to be standing close beside it, picked up the basket and placed it on the table.

"Did you knock it down, Frere, my boy?" asked Mr. West.

"No, sir. It was one of the boarders; I don't know his name. I think he aimed it at some of us, and it fell on the floor instead."

Frere spoke innocently. He had never been to school before, and it did not occur to him that he was doing any harm by his frankness — least of all, to himself! The eyes of his friends and enemies alike glared reproachfully at him, but he did not notice them. It was Jack Brady who broke in.

"We threw the basket at them first, sir, and it did hit them!"

"Well, never do it again, Brady. Look what a mess it's made on the floor! And you others, you have been in the school longer; you ought to have known better than to throw it back. You might have broken something."

That was all. But the bitterness between the two camps was not lessened by the incident, and Frere was liked none the better for it.

However, now work began again, and ill-feeling was shelved perforce for the time. The sarcastic Green, for instance, found himself required to read the part of "Nerissa" to Mason's "Portia"; and Hughes was set to sketch Africa on the board in company with Vickers. The boys did not know that Mr. West had given a hint to the masters to mix the new and old element well together.

That opening day was a weary one to the nine town boys, and all but Jack Brady, the "weekly", scampered off with boisterous delight when school was dismissed at four o'clock.

The two chums, Ethelbert Hughes and Lewis Simmons, had been quickly dubbed "Ethel" and "Lucy", and they did not at once appreciate their new names. But Jack Brady, when he found himself hailed indiscriminately as "Apple" and "Grinner", answered and laughed without a trace of resentment. Perhaps that was why neither title stuck to him, while Hughes and Simmons became Ethel and Lucy to everyone, and even at last to each other.

Jack was standing at the window, watching his friends disappear in the direction of the town, and whistling softly to keep up his spirits, when Hallett approached him.

"Hullo, Red-cheeks, they say you're not a day-boy. I think myself that going home once a week is a mistake; however, of course that's a matter of opinion. But why on earth do you stick by those wretched eight whom West has let in to spoil the school?"

"Fellow-feeling!" Jack's smile atoned for the shortness of his reply.

"Nonsense! I can't for the life of me see why you should connect yourself with that lot at all. We've no quarrel with you."

"Nor with the others, for the matter of that," returned Jack, looking straight into Hallett's face.

Hallett moved away with a short grunt, for want of an answer. Then, remembering one, he turned back.

"What about young Frere? What did you think of that?"

"I'd have stopped him if I could. But he didn't mean any harm. To a home-boy it sometimes comes natural to blurt out all you know when you're asked a question."

Hallett shrugged his shoulders.

"You'll make a first-rate pleader one day, Brady. If ever I want defending, I'll engage you."

"Thanks!" said Jack. "You're very kind."

CHAPTER II. TOPPIN'S DIVE.

If Mr. Anderson, the junior English master, had not happened to meet some friends as he was on his way to the swimming-bath with the boys, this chapter would not have been written. But they were old friends, and very unexpected, who were only visiting Elmridge for an hour or two. So he acted as I suppose nine out of ten young men would have acted in the same circumstances.

"Look here, boys," he said, running after the nearest group. "Can I trust you to go on quietly to the baths by yourselves? I shall follow you very shortly. You can all have your dip, and dress, and by that time I shall be with you. You won't get into mischief, and play pranks, will you? Promise!"

The four boys he addressed promised readily.

"Right! Green, you're one of the seniors; I put you in charge. See that all goes on just as if I were there. No one stay in the water more than twelve minutes."

"Very well, sir!"

And Mr. Anderson departed with light heart and clear conscience.

It was only a couple of days since the term began, and the very chilling reception accorded to the day-scholars had made friendly advances between the two factions next to impossible. A distant toleration was just now the recognized attitude.

But there were two people who were "not playing the game". One was Jack Brady, who persisted in walking first with one party and then the other, and refused point-blank to be distant towards anyone. The other was the youngest scholar of Brincliffe, one Hugill Trevelyan, commonly known as "Toppin". He was only seven, and did not understand the meaning of a civil war. Toppin had been sent to school with his elder brother Escombe because his parents were abroad.

The March Hare (Massimiliano Graglia, to give him once for all his right name), who was two years Toppin's senior, and therefore better able to quarrel to order without knowing the reason why, had a great affection for him, and, when possible, would take charge of him. Toppin being a very independent young man, however, this was not often possible. More frequently he would patronize the March Hare, and explain to him English words or ways that were puzzling.

It chanced that this afternoon three day-boys, Bacon, Armitage, and Simmons, were in advance of the rest of the school, who were sauntering behind in clusters of threes and fours. Hughes was not with Simmons, being forbidden by his doctor to indulge in swimming at present. Bacon looked back just as Mr. Anderson was turning in the opposite direction with his friends.

"Hullo, what sport!" he exclaimed. "Andy's given us the slip!"

"Be joyful! Let's race for the best boxes!" said Armitage. "We shall be in the water long before the other slow-coaches have reached the baths. One, two, three — off!"

Now Toppin was one of the group behind, and being naturally fleet of foot, a race was a thing he could not resist. So he took to his heels and pursued them.

Jack Brady and the March Hare were walking with Toppin, and if it had been practicable, the Hare would have accompanied him in the race, but if there was one thing of which the March Hare was incapable, it was running. Jack, who had found this out, checked him from making the attempt.

"Let Toppin go, Harey, and you stay with me," he said. There was a look of satisfaction on his face. It was fine to see even the smallest boarder chevying three day-boys!

Toppin ran his fastest, and panted into the baths only a yard behind Simmons.

"Why, if here isn't the kid! What the dickens has brought you after us, young un?"

"I saw you — racing," panted Toppin, "and I wanted to see — if I couldn't — catch you. And I did!"

His thick red hair was tumbled by the wind, and the odd little tuft which had won him his nickname stuck up very prominently. The small pink face was aglow with triumph, as he stood gasping for breath, and looking up at the three older boys, his hands planted in his pockets and his feet apart.

"You're a boarder," said Armitage, with a touch of contempt.

"I should think I am! Rather!" was Toppin's proud reply.

"Well, you'd better trot back to your friends, and bathe with them. We're not going to wait for anyone."

"Nor aren't I," said Toppin carelessly.

"Come on!" shouted Simmons from a box. "Don't waste time!"

Preparation for a bath is not a long process with a boy. Garments were dragged off and tossed about, and in a minute they were ready, and dancing round the edge of the clear green water.

Avoiding the steps as a matter of course, Toppin was swinging his arms preparatory to jumping into the shallow end, when, seeing Simmons skipping along the plank that led to the diving-board, in the part where the water was marked "5 ft.", he paused to watch. Simmons raised his hands above his head, curved his body, and dived.

"Oo!" cried Toppin admiringly.

Presently a head appeared, rolling round and blowing. Simmons was swimming towards Toppin. Bacon was now preparing to take a header.

"I say, Lucy, you're not a tall chap. No more aren't I. Why can't I swim and dive?"

"It isn't size that's needed, it's talent," observed Simmons, treading water, as he winked at the little fellow.

"Rot!" said Toppin decidedly. There was a loud splash. Bacon had vanished.

"Up he comes again!" cried Toppin, clapping his hands in an ecstasy. "Oh, I'm going to dive to-day. You can see how easy it is. Let me have a shot before the others come, case I fail."

"Better wait a year or two, Top," said Simmons, deliberately turning a somersault.

"I'm bovvered if I do!" cried Toppin, scampering round to the diving-board. He was in a state of great excitement. "I'm going to dive, and turn head over heels, and stamp in the water, just like you."

"Oh, let the nipper see what he can do!" said Armitage, laughing. He was standing on the diving-board. "There's nothing like beginning early. Can you swim, kiddie?"

"Not—not far," said Toppin cautiously. "I can swim with my arms all right, only I sometimes put one foot on the ground."

"If you don't swim, you'll sink, you know," explained Armitage. "This is deep water."

"Not so very; only five feet," rejoined Toppin. "I'm not funky. Of course I know *how* to swim. I've watched frogs awfully closely."

"Well, then, up with your hands—same as you saw the other two."

Toppin lifted them high, the tips of his fingers met in the approved style, and he took a long breath. Then, gradually, his hands fell back to his sides, and the breath ended in a sigh. Armitage pushed the child impatiently aside.

"Get away, you silly little coward! I'm not going to waste my time standing over you. Go back to the shallow end, and dance at the ropes. We'll come over and duck you."

Toppin was quivering, but his face flushed crimson, and, thrusting himself forward once more, he laid a hand pleadingly on Armitage's wrist. At the same moment a clatter on the stone stairs told of the approach of section number two.

"Give us one more chance, Armie, please! I promise not to funk it again. Listen, they're just coming!"

"You'll not do it," said Armitage.

"Won't I, though! Look here! count three, and then give me a tiny push."

As Jack and the March Hare entered the saloon they heard Armitage say, "Very well. One, two, three; now go!"

There was a faint, quickly-checked cry, and then a little splash. Toppin was under the water.

The same instant the March Hare—hat, boots, and all—had leapt in, and was fighting his way towards the deep end.

Jack's first impulse was to tear off his coat and follow the Hare's example; but when he saw a little red head appear and immediately be captured, and when he realized that Bacon, Simmons, and Armitage were all swimming to the rescue, he refrained.

Although the March Hare was the first to lay hold of Toppin's crest, the next minute he was himself in need of rescue. The Hare had only advanced to the swimming stage when both hands and feet are absolutely necessary, and the pause to seize his friend had sufficed, when combined with the weight of his garments, to sink him; so Toppin dived for the second time, in company with the March Hare.

"Quick!" yelled Jack, "or there'll be two drowned! Shall I come?"

But the pair had risen again, and were clutched and violently wrenched apart by Armitage and Bacon. For the March Hare's grip of the red locks was very tight.

Bacon found Toppin fairly easy to land, but the Hare, in full walking costume, was quite another matter, and Simmons's help was required. Besides, Toppin kept quiet when commanded to, while the March Hare fought and struggled, and had to have his head thumped severely. Fortunately the steps were not far off, and Jack awaited them there.

He was frightened when he saw that Toppin's familiar little pink face had changed to an ivory-white, and that his eyes were shut. Was he senseless, or worse? Jack grasped the small, dripping body in his arms, and staggered to where the bell hung that summoned the attendant. He pealed it loudly, and sank down beneath it to wait. Other boys had arrived during the incident, and were now pressing round, questioning and jabbering. Jack had nothing to say to them. He was hard at work chafing the motionless form, and his brain was in a whirl. What if Toppin never moved or spoke again!

Suddenly the eyelids lifted: Toppin looked straight into Jack's face.

"May I move now?" he asked innocently. Oh, what a relief it was to hear his voice!

"You young fraud!" exclaimed Jack; but his own voice shook, and he was glad to surrender his charge into the hands of the attendant, a man trained for his position. The March Hare, who was shivering beside him, sobbed with joy when he saw one small leg draw itself up, and an arm move a few inches, at their owner's will.

"Top-peen! Top-peen!" he cried. "You are not died!"

Toppin stared at his friend over a tea-spoon. He was sipping hot spirits-and-water, and wondering what it was. But Jack turned upon the March Hare.

"We shall be standing you head downwards in a minute, Hare. You're next door to drowning yourself. Get up, and come with me!"

The Hare protested feebly, with chattering teeth. But the attendant thrust a spoonful of Toppin's drink between them, and counselled Jack to take him to his wife. That good woman stripped the Hare in a twinkling, wrapped him in a blanket, and set him before her kitchen fire to watch his garments dry. Jack meanwhile returned to the saloon, to find Toppin clothed once more, and curled up on the matting, near the heating apparatus, munching a biscuit.

"How do you feel now, Top?" he asked, stooping to see his face.

"Pretty bobbish, thanks, Brady," was the answer, and it told that Toppin was himself again.

"You'll have to look sharp if you want a dip, Brady," called Green. "Andy'll be round in a minute, I expect."

"Thanks! I'm not bathing to-day," was the response.

Just then Escombe Trevelyan, who was swimming lazily about, landed at the steps close by, and beckoned Jack to come nearer.

"I want to hear the truth of this affair, Brady," he began in a confidential undertone. "Did you see it happen?"

"Which part? I saw the March Hare leap in with his hat on his head and his towel on his arm. He did look properly mad, I can tell you!"

"I mean before that, when Toppin went under."

"They say he actually took a dive from the board, don't they?"

"Yes, but I want to get hold of someone who saw it. I can't understand his being such an absolute little fool, and I can't worry the kid himself about it just at present."

So saying, Escombe swam off once more.

Armitage was the next to approach Jack. He looked rather pale, but began by talking rapidly about a paper-chase that was being planned. Jack knew well enough that this was not what he wanted to talk about, but he walked away from the bath with him, still pleasantly discussing starts and times, till they found themselves alone on the stone stairs. Then Armitage came to a stand-still, and his tone changed.

"Brady, I want to speak to you; I want to explain, you know, about Toppin."

"Oh, I saw you push!" remarked Jack bluntly.

"I'm not going to deny it, but do you know that he begged me to? You came in too late to hear that."

"If I hand you a pistol and ask you to shoot me, will you do it?"

"Don't be a fool, Brady. There was no danger. I shouldn't have let him drown."

"He precious nearly did."

"That was the March Hare's fault. I shouldn't have let him sink again."

"Then you think you were right to push him in, Armitage? I don't. Shall we ask Anderson's opinion?"

"No, Jack, I beg and implore you to keep it dark. Of course I should never do it again. But Simmons and Bacon have sworn not to bring me into the affair. Toppin knows it was his own fault, and is a bit ashamed of it. There's only the March Hare besides yourself. I thought perhaps you might persuade him —"

A shadow darkened the open entrance. There was a stamping on the door-mat, and then Mr. Anderson appeared on the stairs. Jack advanced to meet him.

"Finished your bath, Brady?"

"Yes, sir. I mean, I haven't had one. All the rest have. I wanted to tell you there's been a little — a little commotion, sir."

"What on earth do you mean? Not an accident?"

"No, sir; only it might have been. Toppin — little Trevelyan, that is — got into the deep end, and the March Hare — you know the boy I mean, sir — he thought he was drowning, and jumped in after him with his things on, and so they had to haul them both out. Toppin's as right as a trivet again, and as warm as a toast. And the Hare isn't hurt either, but he has to sit in a blanket and wait for his clothes to dry."

Mr. Anderson looked very agitated, and his voice betrayed his feelings.

"Why couldn't you behave as if I was with you? Really, it is absurd to think that all you elder lads can't manage to keep an eye on the juniors for twenty minutes. Where are these two boys? Take me to them directly! What do you suppose Mr. West will say? He'll certainly be extremely angry with you all. I shouldn't be surprised if he stops your coming here."

"We wondered whether you would feel obliged to tell him, sir," said Jack thoughtfully. "Of course, if you must, you must; but it doesn't seem as if there was much to be gained by it, does there? The March Hare and Toppin have learnt their lesson pretty thoroughly."

Mr. Anderson frowned and bit his finger, and the toe of his boot tap-tapped on the ground. It was evident he was undecided. Presently he looked at Jack.

"You mean that, provided I find these two lads absolutely none the worse for their ducking, you beg me, as a great favour, not to carry a report to Mr. West?"

"Yes, sir," Jack responded briskly.

"Well, I won't promise, but I'll think it over."

Mr. Anderson's thought ended in a decision which he announced to the boys when they were gathered together.

"For once, and once only, I have consented to spare you all from certain punishment by not reporting to Mr. West this accident, which you ought to have prevented. But you must never ask or expect to be shielded by me again. Now we will go for a brisk walk as usual, and call for Graglia and

Trevelyan minor on the way back. I dare say they will be ready for us by that time."

Now, none of the boys, except those immediately concerned in the accident, had realized that they were in any danger of punishment; but when the matter was set before them in this light, their gratitude to Mr. Anderson was profound.

"Oh, thank you!"

"Thank you, sir, very much!"

"It sha'n't happen again, sir!"

"Thank you awfully, sir!"

Pleasure and surprise were equally mingled in the boys' expressions. But Jack caught a murmur from Cadbury, very soft and low,

"It's six for us, and half a dozen for yourself, eh, Andy?"

CHAPTER III. THE CHICKEN AND THE BICYCLE.

Mr. West, the master of Brincliffe, was a man of independent mind, and though the boys liked him well enough, there was a difference of opinion regarding his regulations. For example, the same term in which the door was opened to day-pupils, it was shut to hampers, even birthday ones. Cadbury suggested reporting this high-handed act to the Society for the Prevention of Cruelty to Children, but decided to let him off when a permission was announced which almost atoned for the loss of cakes and preserves. Bicycles were allowed!

Every boy who had one might bring it to school, although, of course, there were strict limits to its uses, and he who misused the privilege laid himself open to the heavy penalty of leaving it at home the next term. The plan worked well, and gave huge pleasure to the pupils.

With the exception of such small fry as the March Hare and Toppin, nearly every boy managed to possess himself of a machine of some kind. Many were old, one was originally a lady's, and another had a solid tyre, but so long as the wheels would go round nothing mattered. And the wheel must be in a sorry condition indeed which a boy can't work.

The season was still early when the Bicycle Paper-chase was proposed and arranged. It was Jack Brady's suggestion, and every boy to whom it was named jumped at the idea. Mr. West granted permission, provided that a master accompanied them, and Norman Hallett drifted into the post of captain.

It was agreed, after much consultation, that Hallett and Jack should be the hares, that three minutes' start should be allowed, and that everyone who liked to should be a hound. Simmons was to carry the horn and "blow the true trail" whenever it was lighted upon. Half a dozen more were selected to test the side tracks, as there were certain to be plenty of false scents started.

The Saturday fixed for the chase proved a fine one, and the whole pack was assembled out side the school gates at the hour appointed. Mr. Anderson was once more in charge of the party. Little duties like these fell naturally to his lot as the junior master.

One or two youngsters, who had not got machines of their own yet, had begged leave to hire for the afternoon, so it happened that the March Hare and Toppin were the only boarders left behind. Mournfully they swung upon the gate, and watched the pack ride gaily away at the word "Time!" from Mr. Anderson.

"I wish that they should have tooken us, eh, Top-peen?" said the March Hare.

"You ought to say 'took', not 'tooken'," corrected Toppin. He felt rather cross, and disinclined to dwell on the subject of his wrongs.

"Ah, I am — what is your one word? — non-grammar-eesh?"

"No, — stupid," said Toppin.

"*Uhéi!*" This sorrowfully. Then, drawing nearer, "But no mind! I love you — oh, yes, I love you a great well, Top-peen! Shall we — shall we keess?"

Toppin shook his head decidedly, and jumped off the gate in a hurry.

"That's the second time since Sunday you've wanted to kiss, and I've told you over and over again I hate it, I don't like it! I never want to kiss! Now, do you understand?"

The March Hare was sadly afraid he did.

"If you were an English boy you'd never think of asking such a thing," Toppin went on, tramping up and down as he talked. He really did not want to be unkind to the Hare, but requests like this vexed him sorely. "Don't you see, Harey, there are some people who will kiss me, and I can't stop them — like Miss Turner, f'r instance." Miss Turner was the matron. "And then there are some I've got to kiss, like aunts and people. But one doesn't put in any extra, if one can help it. When I'm grown-up I sha'n't have to kiss anybody, and that'll be jolly. I shall never, never kiss at all, only shake hands or bow, like Escombe does."

"Top-peen, you did keess me once time, last week!" The Hare was timidly reproachful now.

Toppin stood still and coloured.

"Yes, I did. Because you bovvered me to, and—and you'd jumped in after me!"

"And shallent you—not ever—keess me once time more?"

"Oh—well—look here! Perhaps when it's your birthday, if we get somewhere quite secret, where nobody can possibly see us, I—I'll let you have one—a quick one!"

"T-thanks you!" said the grateful Hare.

"It's 'thanks', or else 'thank you'," corrected Toppin.

The Hare took no notice. He only tucked his arm affectionately into Toppin's, knowing that he was keeping within his rights in doing so. Toppin could say nothing. Arm-in-arm is quite correct and English!

"I have som-ting to say. Zat Armitage—he did not ought to be gone chasing paper. He is bad! I hate him, don' like him!"

"Why?" enquired Toppin, with wide-open eyes.

"Be-cause he try to drown you. I am—what is it?—to re-venge it!"

"What awful rot you talk!" said Toppin. "He only did what I told him, same as you would have done."

"Oh no, he had ver' wickedness. Ever'body say he had. I am telling many—one after one, by secret! And he is a debboy. Zey are more angry for zat. So much better!"

"Rubbish!" cried Toppin impatiently. "You've no business to tell anyone anything. And you're looking fierce and ugly, Hare. Do put Armitage out of your head, and come and have a see-saw!"

The chase, meanwhile, had opened well. The track was unmistakable to begin with, and it led right away from the town into the free country. The pack of hounds spun gaily along at full tilt, and many a machine was travelling at a pace it had not known for years. Every now and then there was a small collision, ending generally in a tumble; but if anyone was hurt, he kept it to himself, for all remounted and rode on, and nobody waited behind to make enquiries.

Of course there were any amount of false alarms, shouts and shrieks, wavings and ring ings, and Simmons's toot-toot sometimes went unheard in the hubbub. Mr. Anderson grew quite boyishly excited, and kept bawling, "Come on, you fellows, come on! Buck up! We'll run them down yet!" And it is probable that Mr. West might have had a word to say had he seen the pace at which the willing hounds obeyed.

After one of the collisions above-mentioned, Grey, who was not a good rider, and happened to be the last of the pack, came upon Cadbury, dismounted, by the roadside.

"What's up?" he cried, as he swayed laboriously past.

"Oh, that you, Grey? Get down, there's a good fellow, and hold my bike a jiffey. I'll tow you up the next hill, if you will. Thanks so much! I had a spill just now, and my handlebar's got slewed round, and I can't keep it straight and right it at the same time."

The spanner had to be hunted out, the screw loosened, and the bar straightened; and thus a little time was occupied.

"Bother it! They're out of sight!" cried Cadbury when both were once more ready to mount. "I suppose we shall see Andy tooling back soon, to whip in the lazy pups! Never mind, I'll keep you company. Don't you burst your wind! We'll take it quietly."

"How they do yell! They've lost the trail," remarked Grey. "Hi! I say, there's paper down this lane; look—and it has a bit of Green's writing on it. You bet this is the true trail, and that the hares only scooted along the main road a bit farther, on purpose to mislead."

"You may be right. Anyhow, let's try our luck. It's downhill, so we can put on steam. What sport if they all have to turn round, and find we're in front instead of behind! Mind, old chappie, I'm passing on your right ... wait for you ... below!"

The last words came faintly back; Cadbury had passed Grey like a streak of lightning, his feet up, and his hands in his pockets.

There was a turn in the lane farther down, so that Grey for a minute lost sight of his comrade. He looked carefully ahead as he rounded it, to see if the end of the descent were near. The hill only grew steeper, but the end was a good deal nearer than he thought.

A half-grown chicken, startled by his silent approach, sprang out of the hedge and fluttered in front of his wheel, clucking madly. Grey pealed his bell, but it had no effect on the distracted chicken, which seemed bent on destruction. He clutched his brake; it would not work. There came a stifled squawk, and a slight bump!

In affright and agitation, Grey turned his machine into the hedge, and tumbled off, somehow, anyhow, into the road.

Five minutes later, Cadbury was toiling back up the hill in quest of his school-fellow, when he came upon a very unexpected sight. A prostrate bicycle beside a live, but bruised and dusty boy, who was sadly gazing upon the body of a chicken.

"My good Grey! Good gracious! What has happened? How did you manage it?"

"Oh, Cadbury, I'm so glad to see you! Isn't it awful? I wouldn't have run over it for worlds if I could have helped it, but it simply insisted on it!"

"Suicide while temporarily insane," put in Cadbury, covering his mouth with his hand.

"Well, it did look just as if it wanted to die! But what shall I have to fork out, do you suppose? Five bob? I've got no more on me. Say, they aren't likely to prosecute, are they?"

Grey was really frightened. Cadbury looked at the picture again, tried to take it seriously, failed, and burst into a fit of laughter.

"Awfully sorry, Grey, but—ha, ha, ha!—what am I to do? You—ha, ha, ha!—you do look a treat! I—ha, ha, ha!—I'll stop in a minute. Oh, ho, ho, ho, ho, ho!"

Poor Grey felt anything but amused. He gathered himself to his feet, and remarked stiffly, "Well, Cadbury, when you've done—"

Cadbury steadied himself with an effort.

"It's all over now, Grey. I'm as grave as a judge. And to show you how penitent I am, I'll see this job through for you. But you must obey me to the letter. No, don't brush yourself! Just lie down again as you were, and, however much you're tempted to, don't apologize! Be dignified and injured."

Grey objected, but was persuaded to submit.

"Now to find the owner of this giddy young fowl! We'll see if they lay claim to it here."

Cadbury pushed open a little gate, and knocked at the door of the nearest cottage. It proved to be the residence of the chicken's mistress, an untidy, heavy-looking woman, who apparently lived alone. Cadbury greeted her with the air of a constable, lawyer, and magistrate rolled into one, and the woman listened with deep respect.

"If the fowl of which I am speaking does belong to you," he pursued, in stern and solemn tones, "I am sorry to tell you it has been the cause of a most unfortunate accident that might have proved fatal. I suppose you are well aware that cattle, poultry, and other domestic animals are required to be kept under proper control. If you will kindly step outside with me, I will show you what mischief has been done."

The woman, looking much concerned and a little frightened, followed Cadbury meekly to the scene of disaster. When she saw the lifeless chicken, she raised her hands in horror.

"Dear, dear, dear, sir! Why, it's dead!"

"And it's a very good thing, madam, for you and for all of us, that my friend here is not dead," said Cadbury reprovingly. "The chicken did not die until it had done its best to kill him. And also to wreck his machine! A bicycle is a very costly thing. Grey, my dear fellow, are you feeling a little better? You are sure no bones are broken?"

Cadbury's voice was full of tender anxiety.

"I think not, thanks," responded Grey without moving.

"Dear, dear, dear, sir!" exclaimed the woman again. "Is there anything I can do for you? I'm sure I'm very sorry; I am that!"

"I'm sure you are," said Cadbury, softening towards her. "And we should be most unwilling to take proceedings, or anything like that, if we can only arrange things comfortably."

At mention of the word "proceedings", the woman grew visibly more uncomfortable. She pressed them to enter her cottage, and plied them with plum loaf and unripe gooseberries!

"You see, sir, I'm not so well up as I might be in law matters. Maybe you're right, I won't say. It's hard to keep the chickens from straying, but I'll mind 'em better in future, for their sake and my own too. There's nobody regrets the haccident more'n I do; but I'm a poor woman, and a fine would fall cruel 'eavy on me!"

"I assure you, we wouldn't be hard on you for anything," exclaimed Cadbury, still more kindly.

"You're very good, sir. I don't really 'ardly know what to suggest, but would the chicken be of any service to you now?"

"The chicken! Well, I'm sure we can't refuse that. What say you, Grey?"

"What on earth should we do with it?" muttered Grey.

"Ah, there is one little difficulty, but only a slight one. Would you add the small favour of roasting it for us, ma'am? We have no convenience for cooking it. We should then call the matter settled, and say no more about it."

"Thank you kindly, sir. I'll roast it, and gladly. And where might I bring it to, sir?"

"Oh, my goodness!" ejaculated Grey under his breath. Cadbury considered a moment.

"I think it will be better to leave it to be called for," he said presently. "We shall probably send someone over next Wednesday."

The woman looked mildly surprised at the suggested interval, but only replied, "Very good, sir. Just when you please. It shall be ready. And this is to go no further?"

"Certainly not. I'm sure you have made all the amends in your power, and we are much obliged to you. Good afternoon! Come, Grey, do you feel as if you could make a start? Lean on my arm, and I will help you."

As the woman, grateful and relieved, closed her door, Grey gazed admiringly at his school-fellow.

"Cadbury, what a clever chap you are! I can't think how you worked it. But I say, what about fetching the thing? Who's going to risk that?"

"You are."

"Me! What do you mean?"

"What I say. Aren't you expecting to visit your godmother next Wednesday?"

"Yes; and what's more, I must! She'd write and ask West why I didn't turn up."

"Oh, you'll turn up right enough! But you'll run over here first."

"She lives bang in the opposite direction."

"Never mind. You'll be an hour or so late for once. You must explain that you were—well, detained! She can make what she likes of that."

"Um! I don't feel over sweet on the job."

"Possibly not; we can't always do what we like. It's your little part in the game. I've done mine for the present. You must hide the chicken away somehow and bring it home, and then I'll have a second innings, and undertake all the risk."

By this time the top of the hill was gained once more. Of course any idea of rejoining the paper-chase had to be given up, but a little brushing and beating made Grey respectable, and he and Cadbury rode home together, to confess to having lost the track, and to await the return of the pack, who, after a capital run, had eventually captured the hares at a most convenient spot—the door of a lemonade shop!

CHAPTER IV. A KNOCK AT THE WINDOW.

By mutual agreement the story of the chicken was kept secret for the present, and the next three days passed uneventfully, except to Jack, whose Sunday at home was no small event, though a weekly one. Lessons were just ended on the following Wednesday morning, and Cadbury was doing monitor's work in the school-room when Grey sidled up to him.

"Hullo, Dapple-grey, you're the culprit I was wanting. These are your things, aren't they?"

"Yes; but I was just going to put them away. You mustn't mark me!"

"You've not forgotten the little call you have to pay this afternoon?"

"I wanted to speak to you about that, Cadbury. It's very difficult for me to do it, you know. What do you say—supposing we leave that chicken alone? I don't want to go after it. And it's my chicken, you know."

"Half of it," replied Cadbury. "You can leave your half behind if you like, but I want mine. I earned it by getting you out of your scrape. Look here, Grey! Here are five—six articles belonging to you. I put six marks against your name, and that's half-way to an imp., unless you do your duty towards that chicken."

"Oh, dash it! Well, what have I to do?"

"You can't carve, can you?"

"Don't know. 'Spect so."

"No, I'm sure you can't. It's an art. I can. So that settles it. I must have the fowl first this evening; cut it up, and send on your portion to your bedroom. Let the March Hare fetch it. He's a noiseless customer."

"That won't do," said Grey. "Hallett wouldn't allow it. Since that last pillow-fight, when his bolster knocked a can over and got soaked, he's been awfully down on larks. He's sworn to lick the first boy who opens the door after the gas is out—and he can do it, you know."

"Very well, I'll send it *via* the window," said Cadbury coolly. "All the same, I don't think you'll find Hallett's above eating it. When you hear the chicken knock, open the window and let it in — that's all."

"Oh, yes, it sounds easy enough to you! But supposing I get the chicken, how am I to bring it into the house without being seen? Suppose I meet West in the hall, or Miss Turner on the stairs, or the housemaid in your bedroom? I defy you to hide a roast fowl about you, and I don't care for getting into rows, if you do."

"My dear Grey, we know you don't," said Cadbury. "You're an adept at escaping them. But you needn't fear for this; I have a way out of the hole. I'll drop a line from our window. You come round beneath it on your return, before you enter the house, and tie the chicken firmly to the end of it. Then, when the right time comes, I can haul it up. And look here, don't let's explain to the other chaps how we came by the chicken. Let's make a complete mystery of it for a day or two, and have a lark over it."

That seemed good fun. Grey gradually allowed himself to be persuaded to perform his part of the task. Cadbury, in his turn, made what small preparations seemed necessary. He upset a salt-cellar at dinner, and managed to collect at least half the contents in his handkerchief. He also made a collection of string, chiefly from the smaller boys, who give without asking questions — or, at least, without demanding answers.

Evening came at length, and with it Grey's return. A wink and a nod was all the communication that passed between him and Cadbury, but it satisfied the latter that the chicken was in the garden, and for once he longed for bed-time. In such a hurry was he when the happy hour arrived, that he forgot to wait for Mr. West's departure, and was half-way upstairs when he was called back with a rebuke for his breach of manners.

In the room over which Escombe Trevelyan was head slept also Cadbury, Vickers, Jack Brady, and Toppin, the last-named being despatched to bed an hour before the rest.

"What's up, Cadburius?" enquired Trevelyan with an amused smile. "Got to catch a train?"

"No, a chicken!" was the reply.

"Poor fellow, his mind's giving way!" said Jack.

"Talking about chickens," broke in Vickers, "I saw the old cat sneaking along just now with what looked for all the world like the leg of a fowl in her mouth. You bet the masters are having a tuck-in to-night."

"Not a bit of it!" exclaimed Cadbury. "Depend upon it, she's been at our chicken. The shameless, thieving beast!"

"At yours, Cad?" This was uttered in chorus.

"At mine — ours! It's a treat for us all. I was going to wait till lights were out, but I daren't now. The cat'll have the rest if we aren't quick; perhaps she's eaten it already. Keep cave by the door, Jack, while I haul in the line."

Few things really astonish a boy. Cadbury was regarded as capable of anything, and when the sash was cautiously raised, and the string pulled up, the fact that a real roast chicken, half-wrapped in newspaper, dangled at the end, caused more amusement than amazement.

"Well, I'm blowed! Where did this grow?"

"I shall drop a line to-morrow — two lines — and see what comes up."

"It'll be the old cat, likely."

"Hush! I must stow this away till Pepper's been round," said Cadbury, hastily stuffing the bird into his own bed.

There was not long to wait; Mr. Peace appeared almost before they were ready for him. Mr. Peace was the senior resident master, whose short temper had won for him the above nickname. His back was scarcely turned, the boys were still responding cordially to his rather gruff "Good-night", when Cadbury drew the chicken forth and waved it triumphantly in his hand. Trevelyan, who was next the window, pulled the blind up silently. It was a brilliant moonlight night, so that gas was unneeded.

"The cat has had her full share," Cadbury remarked sadly. "But never mind. Half the chicken belongs to Gr—, to the next room, I mean, and as I've got the trouble of carving, I shall give them the Pussy-half. It'll be all right, they won't know; they'll only think I cut it rather roughly."

"And our reluctance to share supper with the cat is purely a matter of sentiment," added Vickers. "'Where ignorance is bliss, 'tis folly to be wise.'"

"There goes Chickabiddy!" exclaimed Jack, as the fowl suddenly sprang from Cadbury's bed into the middle of the floor. He hopped out and recaptured it.

"Thanks! Well, it's no easy job, I do assure you, to divide a fowl on a bed, with no plate, no fork, and only a penknife. I can carve well enough under civilized conditions, but—"

"Tell us how you came by it, old man," said Jack, who was trying to decide in his own mind whether he should consent or refuse to join the feast. He liked chicken very much indeed, and what would they think if he declined it! Besides, there was no rule against eating chicken in the bedrooms. True, there was something about "No eatables to be taken upstairs". But then the chicken had not been taken upstairs; it had come by a lift. Still, Jack could not quite quiet the little voice within.

"No, I won't shock you with details," replied Cadbury mischievously. "Perhaps you wouldn't eat it if I did."

"I'm not going to anyhow, thanks very much," returned Jack with sudden determination. "There'll be all the more for the rest of you, won't there?"

"Don't talk nonsense!" exclaimed Trevelyan. "Of course you'll have some! If I think fit to eat it, you may. Don't play the blameless prig, for goodness' sake!"

"Brady thinks I've filched it," said Cadbury.

"Brady doesn't want a nightmare," rejoined Jack, laughing, "though he thinks it awfully kind of Trevelyan to answer for his conscience."

"You won't refuse the merry-thought—just for luck, Jack!"

"I have too many of my own generally, specially at Pepper's classes."

"Oh, pinch Brady, somebody! He's punning!" cried Cadbury. "There! it's come in two at last!" and he surveyed his handiwork with great pride. "Now to send along the next room's share!"

Wrapping it in the torn newspaper, he tied it to the string once more, opened the window very gently, and after several unsuccessful efforts whirled it thump against the adjoining window, and waited till a pull at the line showed that it was received.

After a few minutes there came a faint whip at their own window-pane, and Trevelyan took in a scrap of paper weighted with a bull's-eye. Seeing there was some writing on it, he struck a match, and read:

You've bagged the biggest half.
Send us some salt.
Please return bull's-eye.
Where's our leg?

In answer Cadbury screwed up a pinch of salt, and scribbled on the paper:

Ask the cat.
Mind you don't leave your bones about.

Needless to say, the bull's-eye was not returned.

The packet was tossed on to the neighbouring sill, and then they settled down to enjoy their meal in peace. It was well that there was not overmuch light, for they could not consume it elegantly. As a matter of fact, they gnawed it in an ogreish fashion, and in such haste that they could scarcely stop to plunge their bones into the salt for a flavouring.

"I suppose you're quite sure this is chicken, Cadbury?" said Vickers presently.

"Quite. Why do you ask?" mumbled Cadbury.

"It struck me as being rather — well, a trifle gamy, nothing more."

"Pretend it's pheasant, then," said Cadbury.

"Mayn't I have a little bit?"

The sleepy voice came from Toppin's bed.

"Certainly not," replied his elder brother promptly. "Chicken at night is bad for little boys — high chicken especially. Tuck your head in, and don't let me hear you speak again, or I'll come to you with a slipper."

Toppin was kept in very strict order by his brother, and the boys, who were used to his methods, made no remark.

Suddenly, in the midst of the cracking and munching, Jack exclaimed in a whisper, "Cave! I hear feet!"

In an instant all the chicken-bones, salt, paper, and penknives were swooped off the counterpanes, and every boy lay flat and shut his eyes.

That same moment, to their untold vexation, a merry peal of laughter rang out from the next room. And the approaching tread of a man's feet, quick and regular, was heard by all.

"The daft maniacs!" growled Trevelyan between his teeth.

Their door was first opened, and Mr. Peace walked in. Of course, he was received with dead silence.

"Now, boys, you needn't feign sleep, because we know you're wide awake. You've been talking, too. Trevelyan!"

"Yes, sir."

"You are head of this room; what's the blind up for?"

"We — we like to see the stars," suggested Trevelyan.

"H'mph! Was it you who laughed just now?"

"Oh no, sir. My brother woke up a few minutes ago, and I advised him to go to sleep."

Nothing could have sounded more innocent, and perhaps Mr. Peace would have moved on without saying any more, but that, even as he turned to go, there came a little crash at the window-pane.

The boys held their breath in suspense. Trevelyan bit his lip till the blood oozed, and Cadbury covered his face with his hands. Even Jack trembled. Only Vickers lay apparently unconcerned.

"I suppose that was a poor bird dashed itself against the window," he murmured.

"Do you, Vickers? I don't," replied Mr. Peace, striding forward. "Ah, your poor bird has cracked the glass, my boy! I will invite Mr. West to come to your window to-morrow to see a star of another kind."

So saying, the master threw up the sash and laid his hand on a small parcel roughly wrapped and tied with string. It did not escape his notice that the string had an unusually long end, which seemed to be attached to something until he wrested it away. The boys felt more uncomfortable every moment.

Keeping the parcel in his hand, Mr. Peace shut the window very deliberately, drew down the blind, and lit the gas. Then he turned the packet over. Scrawled upon it in large printed letters were these words:

BURY OUR BONES WITH YOURS.

Mr. Peace read them out slowly, with a pause between each. Having done so, he looked round at the inmates of the room, surveying them one by one. Then he stooped to inspect Trevelyan's counterpane. At last he opened the parcel, and found what the boys knew only too surely he would find—a handful of well-picked chicken bones. It was a trying moment.

"And where are *your* bones?" he asked presently. There was an awkward hesitation; then Cadbury, seeing there was no escape, replied meekly, "Under our pillows, sir."

"How horrible!" ejaculated the master with a shudder. He walked to a washhand-stand and selected a large sponge-dish. Depositing in it the greasy parcel he was carrying, he handed it gravely to Trevelyan.

"Put all your bones — your chicken bones — in this, please!" he said.

Trevelyan obeyed, and passed it to Vickers, and so the collection went the round of the room, only passing over Toppin, who was asleep, with his arm tossed above his head. Mr. Peace handed the dish to Jack, but he shook his head:

"Haven't got any, sir."

"Who cooked it?" enquired the master.

"I don't know, sir," answered Trevelyan.

"Brady?"

"Nor do I, sir."

"Vickers?"

"Honestly, I haven't the dimmest notion, sir, though it sounds funny to say so."

"I'm glad you can see the fun. I'm sorry to say it sounds to me too much like lying."

"Sir!" Escombe Trevelyan sat up in bed with flashing eyes to emphasize his indignation.

Mr. Peace turned to him, and stamped his foot angrily.

"Lie down, Trevelyan, at once! You dare to speak to me like that! Cadbury, you're the only one I haven't asked. Who cooked this fowl?"

"A woman, sir. I — don't know her name."

"All right! We'll reserve further enquiries till the morning. If you take my advice, you'll all make up your minds to speak the truth then."

Having delivered this cutting speech, Mr. Peace left the bedroom with the bones.

CHAPTER V. THE STORM BREAKS.

Ten of the Brincliffe boys passed a very bad night. The nightmare, at which Jack had jokingly hinted, was unpleasantly real; there was no dispelling it. Everybody knew that everybody around him was wide awake, but nobody felt inclined to speak.

By and by the daylight came, and brought a little more courage with it.

"After all, I don't care two straws!" exclaimed Cadbury abruptly.

"Who do you suppose does?" said Trevelyan.

Vickers raised himself on his elbow.

"I suggest, Cadbury, that you give us no more information than you have done (which is practically nothing) regarding the source of the supper."

"It should have been bread-sauce," put in Cadbury.

"This isn't the time for puns," said Vickers severely. "I was going to add that in our ignorance lies our only chance of safety. There is certain to be trouble over this affair, and there are three or four points about it which seem to aggravate our case. You see, first"—bringing his fingers into action—"it was Pepper who caught us, and he's a Tartar at all times. Would that it had been Andy! Second, West may take it as a reflection on his table. Third—"

"Would you mind going on talking for an hour or two, Vick?" interrupted Cadbury in a drowsy voice. "I find it very helpful and soothing. Of course, if you could sing the words it would be a still more perfect lullaby."

Vickers, mistaking the voice for Jack's, flung a sponge at the wrong head, and relapsed into silence. Jack, roused at this injustice, dipped the sponge into his water-jug, and returned it with force. Vickers ducked, and it exploded against the wall above his head. Cadbury watched and chuckled. The shadow cast by coming events had not quite overwhelmed the boys' spirits.

When they were called, the boot-boy laid a book on Cadbury's bed as he passed. The inside of the cover was found to contain the following words in Grey's handwriting: —

Dear C., — For pity's sake, dress quick, and meet me 5' before the bell in the housemaid's cupboard. There's standing-room. — E. G.

Now, though they had been thrown together in the chicken incident, Cadbury and Grey were not bosom friends, and Cadbury did not feel particularly eager for this interview. But he good-naturedly did as he was asked, and sneaked out of his room five minutes before the bell had rung which formally permitted the boys to leave.

He found Grey already awaiting him in the chosen rendezvous among brooms, dusters, and pails. It is true there was standing-room, but it was dangerous to move. As the cupboard door opened to admit him, it let in enough light to reveal Grey's white, frightened face, and as he pulled Cadbury inside the latter noticed the clammy "frogginess" of his hands. He drew the door to very carefully.

"Good-morning!" said Cadbury. "This is a pleasant spot to meet in. So romantic!"

"Cadbury, how can you joke, when it's all up with us?" Grey's voice was quite hoarse.

"What's the good of looking forward? Seize the flying moment, and suck honey while you may. That's my motto."

"But you think with me; it *is* all up with us?"

"I'm afraid that's about the long and the short of it. Pepper was very hot and red last night, — regular Cayenne, in fact; and I have noticed that Cayenne at night spells Cane in the morning."

"Cadbury, please stop making fun! I — can't bear it. You don't care, but I do. I haven't slept a wink all night."

"Pick up your spirit, then, and pocket your fears. I'll stand by you, and take my full share. We'll brace ourselves together and face the music."

"Oh no, I can't! I can't! I'm younger than you. I never asked the woman for the chicken, and I begged you to let me off fetching it. You can call me a coward if you like; I don't care! I am afraid!"

There was silence for a moment, and then Cadbury spoke, but in an altered voice.

"Do you mean to say that you want me to leave your name out entirely?"

"Y—yes. If I get in a row it'll be mentioned in my report, and I shall catch it at home. I don't believe you feel things like I do. And it was all your doing, wasn't it?"

"Mostly. Very well, I sha'n't mention you, Grey."

And with that Cadbury marched out of the housemaid's cupboard with his hands in his pockets.

Prayers were followed by early prep., and early prep., by breakfast, without a word on the subject uppermost in the minds of so many. The day-boys arrived, and saw at once that something was up, though what they could not make out. But at ten minutes to nine Mr. Peace entered the room with an excited air, and announced that all the boys were to stand together as at drill. Mr. West wished to speak to them.

The head appeared almost immediately, and ordered the occupants of the two rooms, headed by Hallett and Trevelyan, to stand in front.

He began with a short, studied preface about "an unpleasant duty" and "flagrant breach of rules"; then gave a brief *résumé* of what had taken place, and proceeded to personal enquiries.

"Where did the chicken come from? Who brought it into the house?"

Cadbury stood forward.

"So you are responsible for this, Cadbury? Anyone else?"

"No, sir."

"How did you obtain possession of the chicken?"

"It—got run over—and killed—in bicycling. I mean, I was bicycling."

"Did you steal it, then, or buy it?"

"The woman it belonged to gave it to me, sir."

"After you'd run over it?"

"After it was dead, sir."

"And who cooked it?"

"She did, sir."

"Cadbury, Cadbury! how dare you put forward such a story as this? I can't believe a word of it."

"It's true, sir."

"True! that after you had killed a chicken, the owner not only presented you with it, but undertook to cook it for you?"

"Yes, sir."

Mr. West's only comment on this affirmation was a deep sigh.

Further examination failed to make Cadbury contradict himself; but to certain enquiries he politely declined to furnish an answer.

"Was any boy with you at the time who can bear witness to your story?

"Will you give me this woman's address, that I may send for her?

"How did you manage to get the chicken after it was cooked?"

Such questions as these drew forth nothing.

At length Mr. West, without expressing any opinion, passed on to the subject of the cracked window, but he could not persuade any of Hallett's room to own to the accident. He threatened, he even entreated,—in vain. The clock ticked on; it was a quarter past nine, and everyone was very tired of standing, when the enquiry was brought to an end, and sentence pronounced.

Green and another boy named Buckland were complimented on having "wisely and most properly" kept themselves and their respective rooms entirely outside the affair. Cadbury, on his own confession—"an extraordinary, and, I am bound to say, improbable tale"—was to suffer first and worst, and had the doubtful distinction of accompanying Mr. West there and then to his study. Next, the inmates of Hallett's and Trevelyan's rooms were doomed to forego supper for three days, Hallett's room being sentenced in addition to pay for the mending of the cracked pane. Lastly, and this was the part of the sentence that roused the whole school, all— boarders and day-boys alike—were to forfeit the next half-holiday.

The day-boys looked so exceedingly blank at the news that Mr. West added that he included them because, "as long as I can obtain no full confession, I am compelled to regard you, with all your opportunities and freedom, as being as much under suspicion as the rest". He wound up by observing that no doubt it was "the old, hard case of the many suffering for the few", but this did not afford much consolation to his aggrieved pupils.

Of course there was nothing to be said at the time, but as soon as they were alone they fell into clusters, and gave vent to their opinions by storming at one another.

"Abominable!"

"Beastly unfair!"

"The meanest thing I ever heard!"

These were the kind of expressions that floated about the room.

But one small group, of which Hallett was the principal member, instead of reviling the head-master, was expending its wrath upon a fellow-boy.

"The cowardly young toad! Had to do with it, you say? I should think he had, indeed! A good deal more than we've any idea of."

"Well, we know he did the window."

"We do, and he shall have the pleasure of paying for that. He shall, if it empties his cash-box for a year following. Those members of the room who yearn to subscribe may do so."

"He was on the outlook for the chicken, you remember. Of course he must have known all about it. Cadbury can confirm that."

"*Can*, but you don't know Cadbury if you think he will. What I say is, ask the young sneak himself. Put it to him straight, and let's see that we get the truth. Why, we should never have lost our half if he had owned up with Cadbury."

"And it's so jolly rough on Cadbury too! Why should one be licked and not the other?"

"Oh, we'll see to the other if necessary. But let's hear what he says for himself. By the way, where is he?"

Where indeed? A careful search revealed the hapless Grey huddled up in the book-room, terrified and miserable.

"Here he is! Hoping to be taken for the *Treasury of Knowledge*," cried his discoverer, and straightway dragged him into the light. There was a rush to the book-room.

Grey was put to the question, failed to clear himself, found guilty — and licked.

Jack Brady was the centre of another group, which seemed inclined to be angry with him.

"Brady's no business to have his supper stopped," said Trevelyan. "He never touched a morsel of that wretched fowl."

"He ought to have told West so."

"Such nonsense!" exclaimed Jack. "I could have eaten some if I'd wanted to. Now, Toppin's case is different. He wasn't allowed to have any. I vote we sign a petition in favour of him. It will really be hard cheese if he's made to suffer."

"Toppin, here!"

The boy was chanting over his spelling, but he hopped up promptly at his elder brother's call.

"They say they are going to get up a petition to have you let off the sentence for our room, because you didn't eat any chicken."

"Oh, I'd hate to be let off!" exclaimed Toppin. "I know it's because I'm little, and I want to be treated as if I was big like the rest. I'd heaps rather! 'Sides, I would have eaten some chicken if you'd have let me, so it's same as if I had done, isn't it?"

"You hear, Brady?" said Trevelyan with a laugh. "A nice pair of lawyers you'd make! Two exactly contrary arguments are used to persuade us of the very same fact."

"Well, it comes to this, that we want all to share and share alike. Isn't that it, Top?"

Jack tweaked the defiant tuft as he put the question, and Toppin laughed up at him and nodded.

The most unfortunate effect of the whole incident was the bitterness which it revived in the day-scholars. It had almost seemed as if time was breaking down the wall of enmity which was so strong at the beginning. But today's work strengthened it still further. The day-boys had congregated together, and were speaking their minds in tones that were the more seriously angry because they were subdued.

"This is what they wanted, to bring us into trouble; and a lot they care that they're in the same boat!" The theory was Bacon's, and he announced it with confidence.

"It's the spirit of the thing one kicks at — the spite, the injustice! Not the loss of the half!" declaimed Mason with warmth.

"Let's pay 'em out!" said Simmons.

"How, Lew?" Hughes put the question, but all waited eagerly for the answer.

Simmons might be small, but he was brimful of bright ideas.

"Fight," he replied. "We're much fewer, but it would be mostly a matter of siege and stratagem, and if we planned it out, I bet we could give them a wipe-down."

"I mayn't fight," said Frere sadly. "They won't allow me to."

"And I'm awfully afraid I can't," added Hughes.

"What's more, you sha'n't, Ethel!" said Simmons, who was amusingly careful of his friend's health. "There'll be lots of quiet work for you and Frere — scouting and so forth."

"I'm nuts on fighting," put in Armitage.

"As for me, I'm spoiling for the fray," laughed Mason, exhibiting the muscle of his arm with great pride.

"Oh, well, it will teach them to respect us anyway. And that will be something gained," said Simmons. "Mason, will you captain us?"

"Not much! No, I'll do my duty as a lieutenant, but I am no commander. Nor are you. You're too little."

"Napoleon — Nelson!" muttered Simmons. He would have liked the offer of the post, and his size was a sore point with him.

"Jack Brady must be captain," said Bacon firmly, and all agreed with him.

"However could we have forgotten him?" exclaimed Hughes.

"He's the right man, if he'll consent," remarked Mason. "But I wish I felt sure about that."

"Well, I see at the present moment he's hobnobbing with the enemy," said Hughes doubtfully.

"Oh, but he's really one of us, he has been all along," cried Simmons. "Here, Brady, you're wanted."

"At your service," said Jack merrily, and, breaking off his conversation with Trevelyan and Vickers, he joined the group of day-boys.

"Brady, have you heard that they've dragged us into this row? That our half's stopped along with the boarders'? Though none of us ever saw or tasted so much as a drum-stick!"

"None of you? Ever?" put in Jack. "That's a big order, Piggy-wig."

"You know what I mean," rejoined Bacon. "They might have had a swan or a peacock for all we knew about it."

"But, my dear fellow, it's West you must blame. No one mentioned you."

"No, but not one of them had the honesty to stand out and clear us — to assure him we'd nothing to do with it," said Mason. "Instead of that they are careful to turn it into a mystery, on purpose that we may all be suspected."

"Well, well, it's only just a single half that's lost. It'll soon be over and forgotten."

"Will it?" cried Simmons indignantly. "I fancy it will be remembered longer than you think by some. We mean to pay them in full for their mean spite. We're going to unite and fight."

"Oh, challenge them to a cricket match instead! I'll play for you. Think how much more sportive that will be! Not to say, sensible."

"Come, Brady, we're not babies. We mean to make them sorry by force."

"Take care you're not made sorry by force, Lucy!"

"Oh, never fear! The masters won't know anything at all about it if we can help it. We shall pick our opportunity. But look here, Brady, you've got to captain us!"

"Bothered if I do!" said Jack.

"Very well, don't! Go over to the boarders instead, as you want to, and repeat everything we've told you." Bacon spoke angrily.

"Piggy-wig, don't be a fool! If you want me to quarrel either with your set or with the other chaps, I say I won't, and that's flat! You must take me as you find me, and if you're all bent on fighting and making geese of yourselves, I shall just stay as I am — once for all — Jack of Both Sides."

CHAPTER VI. THE MARCH HARE'S REVENGE.

Cling, clang—creak! Cling, clang—creak! So the discordant bell sounded forth in the playground, the interval between the strokes being filled by a harsh, rusty squeak that set one's teeth on edge. The message it bore to the boys was, "Come in—quick! Come in—quick!" For the time was ten minutes to nine, and the day that following the incident which was already known as the Chicken Row.

The monitors this week were Brady, Bacon, and Armitage, and they had already gone in to their duties. The old bell always went on ringing for two minutes, and the boys were in the habit of waiting until it was on the point of ceasing, when they obeyed it with a rush.

But on this particular morning the day-scholars seemed, for some reason best known to themselves, one and all consumed with zeal for their studies. At the first preparatory creak they made a simultaneous dash for the entrance, which caused much mirth amongst the boarders.

Cadbury waved his arm in their direction, and turned up his eyes with an air of mock tragedy, while he spouted with rolling "r's":

"How fair a sight it is to see
Youth lay aside its giddy glee,
Athirst for learning's boundless sea!
How different from you and me!"

"My dear boys," said Vickers, with pretended solemnity, "I require obedience in you, but I desire something more—something which you can give, but I cannot command. That something is cheerful obedience—ready obedience—obedience that hurries gladly at the call of duty. And now that you see a pattern of such obedience, you might do worse than copy it."

His imitation of Mr. West's emphatic voice and rather studied manner was so true to life that it was greeted with a roar of laughter, and for once Vickers had the gratification of seeing his wit appreciated. The very phrase, "you might do worse", was a favourite with the head-master, and one which the boys had long ago selected for mimicry.

But now there came the faint, irregular stroke that foretold the stopping of the bell, and the boys moved quickly towards the entrance, and began to jostle one another in their haste. On reaching the door, however, much fumbling and kicking began.

"Hi, you in front there! Look sharp and go in! We're waiting!" cried Hallett in a voice of angry authority, and pushing commenced in the rear.

"It's no good pushing; it's stuck!" was holloaed back, and the kicking and banging increased in vigour.

"What nonsense! Let me come! It must be opened! Won't Pepper wire into us in a minute!"

Green elbowed his way to the front, and turned the handle violently. Only once, and then he faced round with the exclamation, "You fools! It's locked!"

At which news much breath and a little time were wasted in furious threats towards those by whom they had been tricked.

"Won't they pay for this!"

"West shall hear if they don't let us in sharp."

"I'll knock their heads together when I do get in!"

"The impudent beggars! We'll give them such a lesson!"

But within all was glee and triumph. Simmons and Bacon fairly danced with malicious satisfaction, whilst Armitage and Mason chuckled grimly.

"What'll they do? Go round to the front?"

"They'll catch it if they do."

"We shall too if the joke once reaches West," said Jack. "Don't you think you might wind up the trick now, and let them in?"

"All in good time," said Mason coolly. The banging at the entrance grew terrific, and though separated from the first class-room by a long passage, he had to raise his voice to be heard above it. "Let's be quite sure that we're ready for them. You — Bacon and Armitage — have you done your job?"

"Yes, properly."

"We ought to, for we've been at it nearly half an hour."

"And you others — Brady, Ethel, Lucy, et cetera — you've all got your books ready?"

"Ay, ay, sir," laughed Simmons.

"What was your job, Armie?" asked Jack. He had been engrossed in inking new slates.

Armitage smothered a laugh.

"Muddling, Jack, my boy, muddling! And a truly artistic muddle have we made. It's been a game of 'General Post' with the books. The dictionaries have taken the atlases' place, the Greek grammars have deposed the Latins, and — "

"Hist!" interrupted Jack. "I smell Pepper! We must whistle to Ethel." And without waiting for permission he did so.

"Ethel" was posted down the long passage by the school entrance, with instructions to turn the key back when he heard the signal. The sound of unlocking was drowned in the hubbub without, and, turning, he fled noiselessly up the passage and into the school-room, at the identical moment in which two others made their appearance there — namely Mr. Peace, through the opposite door, and Norman Hallett outside the window!

"Now, then, where is everybody?" cried the fussy little master, seeing less than a dozen boys assembled for work. Then his eye fell on Hallett's pale, angry face peering through the glass. "Why, Hallett outside? What's the meaning of this? What's the meaning of this?"

"Do you think perhaps they didn't hear the bell, sir?" suggested Simmons. "They've been making rather a noise outside."

Mr. Peace was not deceived by the boy's demureness.

"You want your ears boxed, you rogue!" he began; but at that moment in surged a torrent of rather frightened, very wrathful boys, who had been unprofitably spending the last half-minute in striving with penknives to force the lock of the already unfastened door.

However, the rudiments of school honour forbade their furnishing the master with an account of the occurrence, and they had to content themselves with breathing dark threats to those day-boys who crossed their path in the frantic rush to the book-room.

At sight of that rush a few of the milder spirits, such as Hughes and Frere, held their breath in dreadful foreboding, while the unconscious Mr. Peace roared:

"Now, then, how long do you mean to stay in there? The clock's on the strike. I mark every boy who isn't in his place when it stops! Do you hear me? Do you hear me, I say?"

"No," responded Cadbury, without thinking. Then, poking his head out, "What are we to do, sir, please? We can't find our books. Everything is changed. It's worse than a spring cleaning. Won't you look and see, sir?"

Before the invitation could be answered, there was an impatient knock of authority in the school-room—a rap of knuckles upon a desk—and everyone knew what that meant. Mr. West had entered, and was being kept waiting.

With what books they had managed to grab—some the right ones, many the wrong—the boarders slunk red-faced to their places, there to realize their luck, and perchance to discover their mistakes. Cadbury had no book at all. Green found himself hugging Toppin's *Little Reader* instead of *Elementary Physics*; and Hallett might make what use he could of the March Hare's *English Conversation* when he came to open it.

The pages of the masters' registers fairly bristled with black marks that unhappy morning. Grey was for bringing the enemy to book, and reporting his evil devices, but his elders quashed the proposal.

"You silly duffer! As if we couldn't deal with them ourselves. Wait till lunch. There's a rod in pickle for them, and they know it."

Yes, the day-boys had a suspicion that there was a lively time approaching, but so set-up were they by their recent victory that they quite looked forward to it.

Jack was less happy. He read the resolve in the boarders' faces, and knew that they saw no joke in that morning's events. And he wondered where the war would end. It seemed the final upset of all those little efforts towards harmony and good-temper to which he had given himself from the hour of his arrival at Brincliffe.

Among the junior scholars sat a dark-complexioned boy with very white teeth. It was the March Hare. To-day there was a queer gleam in his eyes, and a flush of carmine in his sallow cheeks. His *English Conversation* was not to be found when wanted, and the fact called down upon him a sharp rebuke from a master, but his face expressed no regret.

"There must have been a ringleader in this," remarked another boarder in his hearing during a momentary absence of the master. "I wish to goodness we knew who it was!"

"A reng-lidder?" repeated the March Hare. "I don' know zat word. But if you mean ze boy who done ze much most — ze baddest of all ze bads — ah, I know him! Yes, I mark him long, long time. An' I wait."

"What d'ye mean, Harey? Who is it?"

"Nev-er mat-ter," said the March Hare mysteriously; and at that point Mr. Anderson re-entered the room.

On went the hands of the clock. At one minute to eleven all was peaceful and orderly. At eleven the masters departed for the usual brief interval. At one minute past eleven all was war and tumult!

How, where, with whom the conflict commenced it is impossible to say. There was no warning, no formal outbreak — only in a moment the quiet room became a battle-field, filled with a seething crowd of furious, struggling lads.

An odd feature of the battle was its comparative silence. It was to everyone's interest to avoid attracting attention, and the sound of blows was louder than the sound of voices.

Here, Bacon was felled by Trevelyan; there, Vickers by Mason. The result was the same in either case. The fallen arose undaunted and without a word; only a look of keener determination settled on each face.

There was scarcely time for rallying, but, as far as was possible, the day-boys closed in together to resist the attack of their more numerous foes. Hughes and poor Frere both found themselves forced into battle, willy-nilly. Jack, whose natural instinct was to side with the weaker party, found neutrality impossible, and the part he had chosen very hard. The day-boys were prepared for his vagaries, but the boarders were perplexed and bewildered by his conduct. Was he partisan or traitor? One moment they saw him pressing his handkerchief to Green's bleeding nose; the next he was forcing a way for plucky Simmons to reach his friends: now he must needs shut Toppin up in the book-room for safety — against his will, of course; then he was heard imparting to the tearful Frere a few hints on self-defence.

Very soon there was no doubt in which direction the tide of victory was flowing. Numbers began to tell, and the day-boys were being forced steadily backwards towards the wall, away from the class-rooms, where they had hoped, if necessary, to be able to entrench themselves.

A foolish idea of making use of the long table suggested itself to Mason. A tug and a shove, and they had pulled it round to shield them.

"You lunatics! You're giving them twenty fresh chances at once!" cried Jack desperately. "They can squeeze you into surrendering directly!"

"I believe he's right!" muttered Bacon, and they strove to get free again.

But it was not easy to rid themselves of the table when once they were ranked behind it. The boarders saw their opportunity, and a last fierce combat began.

Something — Jack never knew what it was — suddenly impelled him to dive under the table.

"Oh, Jack, we don't fight underground!" exclaimed Cadbury mockingly; but Jack paid no heed.

Cadbury was wrong; there was a very definite attack being made beneath cover of the table, where it was least suspected. An attack, too, of a kind that would have been thought impossible.

It was very dark under there, but Jack was at once certain that he was not the only hider from the light. A small, lithe figure was wriggling along the floor in front of him, passing one pair of legs after another, but scanning each in turn.

Jack's hand was almost upon it. The words "This isn't fair play!" were bursting from his lips, when the figure ceased to crawl. It was opposite a pair of ribbed brown stockings clothing two sturdy legs, when it stopped, and drew something forth from somewhere about its person.

At sight of this, a chill of horror seemed to freeze Jack, and for the moment he was struck dumb. Stiffly he put forward a hand which seized, as in a grip of iron, the thin right arm of the figure before him. It was the arm of the March Hare, and in its hand was an open penknife.

The sudden clutch was wholly unexpected, and the knife dropped. With his other hand Jack picked it up. As he did so, the March Hare uttered a cry. It was neither loud nor long, but there was something so startling in it that the commotion of the fight ceased suddenly, and in the midst of a strange stillness Jack emerged, dragging his captive by one hand, and holding the open penknife in the other.

If a white flag had been raised, the battle could not have ended more abruptly. For a few seconds nothing was heard but quick, short breaths on all sides. Presently Hallett's voice, hoarse and low, asked:

"What does it mean, Brady?"

Jack, white to the lips, pointed from the Hare to Armitage, then to the spot where he had found him. The Hare was shivering and sobbing.

"Hallett—I hear you say knifes—war wiz knifes! I on'y go to ze Toppeen-drowner. I not wasn' going to hurt—on'y to preeck! I never hol' knife no more! I promise! I swear!"—here he crossed himself rapidly—"I promise 'gain! I—"

But at this point the English language failed the Hare, who sank upon his knees, wringing his hands and gesticulating wildly, as he gabbled, nobody knew what, in Italian.

Hallett, meanwhile, was looking grave and stern as the boys had never seen him. There was not a trace of the fiery tyrant they knew so well. He was face to face with a hard duty, and it awed him.

"I'm sorry," he said quietly, "but this is too serious to be covered up. I have no choice. I must take you straight to the head. Brady, hand me over the penknife! Or bring it along, and come too!"

Jack shook his head as he passed the knife, and Norman Hallett and Massimiliano Graglia left the room in company. Two masters returning met the pair, but Hallett's face wore an expression which forbade questions.

When presently he re-entered the school-room, it was alone.

And for the space of a week the March Hare was unseen by his school-fellows.

CHAPTER VII. HANNAH THE HOUSEMAID.

There was an end of open strife among the Brincliffe boys. The sight of that little glittering blade had brought them up short with an unpleasant shock. They stood astounded for a minute, making no attempt to remove the traces of the conflict, even when they heard the sound of the masters' approach. They stood convicted, all together; their disordered dress, collars unfastened and rumpled hair, the untasted luncheon, the confusion of the furniture, all told most graphically the tale of a quarrel.

Silent and ashamed they slunk back into their places when the head-master at last returned to the school-room. But, to the universal surprise, he only addressed a few short, grave sentences to them on the subject, and announced that henceforth a master would have charge of the room during the luncheon interval.

"Hitherto, boys, I have allowed you considerable liberty, regarding you, though young, as civilized and Christian gentlemen. You have shown me I was mistaken. Therefore I must treat you differently until I see you become what I hoped you already were. You might do worse than strive to attain to this. To your classes, if you please!"

"Does anyone know where Trevelyan minor is?" enquired Mr. Anderson presently, looking into the mathematical class-room.

Jack sprang from his seat.

"Yes, I know! Please, sir," turning to his master, "will you excuse me?"

"No need for you to come, Brady," interposed Mr. Anderson; "tell me where he is, that's all."

Jack hesitated; then, putting his hand in his pocket, drew out a key.

"He's in the book-room, sir. And it's locked."

Now, as the book-room opened out of the school-room, in which Mr. West was teaching, it was impossible that the door could be unlocked, and Toppin released, without the fact becoming known to him. He looked up at sound of the key, and the sight of the small, red-haired urchin, seated disconsolately on a globe within, and swinging his short legs, evoked a question.

"What has that lad been doing, Mr. Anderson? Did you lock him up?"

"No, sir; it was Brady."

"Indeed? And what business had he to take the law into his hands? What were you locked up for, Trevelyan?"

Poor Toppin was feeling very sorry for himself, and distinctly bitter against Jack. He had heard the sound of many interesting things happening, and had a strong suspicion that he had been forgotten. Aware that he had not merited such hard treatment, he now replied plaintively:

"Nuffing at all, sir!"

"Well, in any case, I have not yet given his training over to Brady," observed Mr. West dryly, and without further question Jack was sentenced to twenty minutes' detention at twelve o'clock, "to see how he liked his own treatment".

"Rough on you, Jack of Both Sides!" said Simmons, as he passed him on his way into the open air. "Your policy's fine in theory, but I'm afraid it won't pay. Jack of Both Sides, friend of neither, eh?"

Jack's reply was quite cheerful:

"Not so bad as that, thanks, Lucy. We're going to be friends all together, the whole boiling of us, before we've done!"

"Think so?" said Hughes, and shrugged his shoulders. "Not much chance of that yet, I'm afraid. I spoke to Hallett just now, and he wouldn't even answer me."

Jack seemed out of luck's way this week, for the next morning he had an accident with the ink, was fined sixpence for breaking one of the pots, and ordered upstairs to change his bespattered garments.

Just outside his bedroom, in the passage, he came upon one of the housemaids, in front of whom, on the ground, lay a pillow and a heavy overcoat.

"Hullo, Hannah! Having a pillow-fight with an overcoat, for fault of a live enemy, eh? I've caught you in the act! Now, I want you to do something for me. I've been taking an ink shower-bath, you see, and I go home to-day, and I must wear this jacket. Could you—"

But there Jack stopped short, for Hannah had broken into his sentence with a jerky little sniff which he felt pretty sure was a stifled sob.

"Why, my good Hannah, what's up? I'm most awfully sorry if there is anything wrong. Do tell us what it is!"

"Oh, well, Master Brady, I'm sure it isn't your doing, but it's one of the young gentlemen, and I don't mind which, but I do think it's very ill-mannered and unkind, and I've always tried to do my duty by you all, and more than that sometimes; and it's turned my thumb-nail back and broken it, and the big buttons banged in my face, and dragged my hair down; and it's no pleasure to do it, but I shall 'ave to carry the tale to the master—"

"A booby-trap, I suppose," interposed Jack, looking thoughtful.

"Well, sir, a trap—that's certain, for I walked in through the door as innocent as a child; but I don't see on that account that I'm to be set down for a booby."

"No, no; it's only the name for the trick," Jack hastened to explain, for Hannah was looking more hurt than ever. "You balance the pillow on the door, you know—and it needs some care, because it might fall the wrong way, don't you see, and never hit you at all; and adding the overcoat must have made it more difficult."

There was an unconscious tinge of admiration in Jack's voice, and Hannah did not seem entirely consoled. As he handed her his stained jacket, however, he added: "You know, it wasn't meant for you, Hannah. You got it by mistake. It was put up for Frere; I'm sure of that. On these mornings he always comes to this room first thing to practise his violin. Whoever set the trap never thought about you, that's certain."

"That don't matter, sir, it hurt me just as much," persisted the maid. "And they've no business, 'aven't the young gentlemen, to play pranks like this. You never know what you'll be let in for next. I shall be in a heverlasting flutter now. It's worse than living in a monkey-house."

"Have you ever tried that, Hannah? I shouldn't have thought this was actually worse; but of course when one's tried both — "

"Master Brady, you're teasing me, and you know my meaning quite well." Hannah's voice was positively tearful, and Jack grew alarmed.

"Nonsense! I wouldn't tease you for the world. But look here, I want you to think better of what you said — about carrying the tale to Mr. West. There's an awful lot done by passing things over; you don't know! Let's return these articles — see, it's Cadbury's pillow and Trevelyan's coat, so neither of them set the trap — and let's agree to forgive and forget for once. Won't you?"

Jack could be very gentle and persuasive, and Hannah's heart was not proof against his pleading.

"Well, sir, just this once, since you put it like that, and hask so particular."

"There's an angel! I knew you would. You come to me, Hannah, when you're in any fix, and see if I don't repay you for this. Hullo! here's Frere and his fiddle. I'd better scuttle."

"Yes, Brady, I think you had better," observed Frere. "I heard Mr. West asking for you."

"Ugh! I never like being asked for," remarked Jack, and straightway vanished.

"So peace isn't signed yet," he said to himself. "The campaign has only changed its character, for secret and irregular warfare. I don't seem to have accomplished much so far."

Jack went home that Saturday feeling rather discouraged. He little knew what his accidental interview with Hannah, the housemaid, would result in.

He was flinging his own and Trevelyan's muddy boots into the big basket which stood in the scullery, on Monday evening, when a low voice close at hand startled him.

"Please, Master Brady, if you have a minute to spare, I should like to speak to you."

Jack turned round in surprise, to face his friend of Saturday, the housemaid.

"Why, certainly. Fire away! I'm all attention."

"I hope you won't think me foolish, sir, but you—you do seem sympithetic like, though you can't help me, I know; and yet you told me to come to you, and it's a relief to out with one's trouble; and Emma, she don't understand, because she's going to be married, and she don't think of nothin' else; and Cook, she says she's never 'ad nothin' to do with plants, not excep' the eatin' sorts, like cabbages and turnips—"

"But, Hannah, you haven't given me a chance yet. Plants?" said Jack.

"Yes, sir; I'll tell you all about it if I may. You see, my 'ome's at Brickland—that's a matter of four miles from Elmridge,—and my father, he's steadily wastin', and doctor says there's no chance for him, not unless he gets to one of the hopen-air 'ospitals, and he's not to doddle about the green-'ouse any more."

"That's a bad business," said Jack, looking grave. "Then your father has been a gardener?"

"Yes, and a salesman in a small way, sir. But now he's to give up, and sell all the plants. Doctor says he'll never again be fit for that work. It's goin' in and out of the cold and the heat and the damp that's so tryin'. He's been holdin' on as long as he could, but now he's ready enough to part with 'em, and if only he could get a good price it'd maybe take 'im to the hopen-air, and help to keep the 'ome together till he's well."

"That sounds the wisest plan," observed Jack thoughtfully.

"Yes, sir, but the point is the sellin' of 'em. They ought to go into a good big sale, where there'll be plenty of biddin'; they aren't enough in themselves to draw buyers. And Mother says in her letter this mornin' they've heard of one that's bein' held in Elmridge on Saturday, a big one, in the Rookwood grounds. They call it a 'Nurserymen's Combine'; there's a many of them joining, and they're willin' to take in Father's little lot."

"Surely the very thing!" said Jack.

"It seems so, doesn't it, sir? Father he sent round at once to make arrangements. But what do you think? he can't get the carting of 'em done under three-and-six a load; and, as he says, he hasn't got half a guinea to lay out that way. Why, it'd pay his train to the hopen-air! So 'e'll have to let it slide, and not get such a chance again in a hurry."

"I'm sure I'm awfully sorry about it," responded Jack feelingly. "But—but—but keep up your spirits, and who knows what may turn up?"

And with this consoling advice, he turned on his heel.

CHAPTER VIII. JACK'S MAIDEN SPEECH.

"You really wish me to understand, Brady, that not you alone, but all the elder boys—day-pupils and boarders alike—desire of your own free-will to devote your next Saturday's half-holiday to conveying this poor man's plants from his house at Brickland to the Rookwood sale?"

"Yes, sir, that's what we want to do."

"H'm! Well, the proposal does you credit, and you certainly might employ your time much worse than in carrying it out. I don't think it would be right for me to refuse your request. Mr. Anderson, I feel sure, will be ready to help and advise you, if necessary, but as the idea is your own I should like you, as far as possible, to carry it out by yourselves."

"Thank you, sir!" said Jack, and withdrew.

It was evening when this dialogue took place. The day-boys had departed in an irritable frame of mind, on account of various annoyances of which they had been the victims during the past two days. Bacon had been tripped up twice by a piece of string, Hughes had found his coat-sleeves tightly sewn up with packing-thread, and Simmons's pockets had been crammed with moist, wriggling earthworms.

Knowing this, it may be wondered that they were prevailed on to agree to Jack's scheme for the coming Saturday. But our hero was wily, and he worded his suggestion so carefully that they did not for a moment imagine that their enemies the boarders were at all connected with the plan, which seemed to offer scope for fun and adventure of a new description. Was not Saturday Jack's regular day of release? Of course this was to be an "out-of-school" affair altogether. So they imagined.

"Now then, you fellows!" cried Jack, bursting into the school-room like a frolicsome whirlwind, "who said I wouldn't get leave? West and I have settled it all most comfortably, patted each other on the head, and so forth. Let you go? Why, he'd like nothing better than to let you go for good and all!"

"So you've let the whole lot of us in for it, young man?" said Trevelyan, looking amused.

"Why, nobody asked to be left out," returned Jack.

This was quite true, and there was no more to be said. Hallett had taken kindly to the idea to begin with, and set the fashion by doing so. One or two lazy lads would not have been sorry in their hearts if Mr. West had vetoed the scheme, but they had not the courage to refuse to join in it.

"Now to business!" Jack continued. "We must send Mr. Thompson himself word of our intentions; let's write a proper, tradesman-like letter! Vickers, you're the fluent, flowery one. Bottle up your metaphors and give us a page of business-like fluency! Here's some paper."

After a good deal of discussion the following letter was composed: —

To Mr J. Thompson Nurseryman.

Dr Sir/

Having heard of yr intention to dispose of yr stock-in-hand (Plants) we have pleasure in proposing to undertake transport of same (carriage free) on Saty next ensuing between 2 and 4 p.m. from yr house to Rookwood Elmridge Middleshire for sale advd to be held there at 6 p.m. Safety of goods guarantd. Unless we hear to contry we shall presume this meets yr views and take action accordly.

Yrs etc.

(Signed)
T. Vickers
N. Hallett
J. Brady &c.
pro) Students of Brincliffe Elmridge.

"If that isn't business-like, I don't know what is!" exclaimed Cadbury, when it was read through. "If ink was a shilling a drop, you couldn't have been more chary of it. There's not an 'a', 'an', or 'the' throughout, nor a comma, nor an adjective, and the contractions are masterly. We're all born commercial clerks, that's what we are!"

"Ethel and Lucy have undertaken the necessary barrow-borrowing," remarked Jack, casually. "We sha'n't want more than six or eight wheel-barrows, and that pair can get anything if it goes together. Lucy represents the dauntless cheek, and Ethel the irresistible charm. What more is required?"

"What do you mean, Brady? We won't have the day-boys sticking their fingers into this pie!" cried Escombe Trevelyan.

"We couldn't do the job alone," said Jack quietly. "It would take us twice as long."

A loud murmur of disapprobation ran through the room.

Jack turned rather pale, and pinched the edge of the table nervously. His eyes wandered from face to face. All were vexed, all displeased. Then, with a sudden impulse he sprang to his feet, and spoke his mind—rapidly, earnestly.

"Look here, I can't understand it! What makes you all so beastly to the day-boys—to my pals? You began it, not they! They came to Brincliffe without the least idea of any unfriendly feeling, and you hated them before you'd seen them or heard their names. Is that fair—straight—English? If it were, I'd wish to be French or German. Where's the fun in this constant worrying of each other? As boarders, it's your place to put out a hand first, and I think I can promise that the day-boys will shake it. Bah! I know I can never talk you round; it's no good attempting to. I'm not in a comic mood, and can't make you laugh, like Cadbury, and I haven't Vickers's gift of the gab. But wasn't last Friday's lesson enough? Wasn't the sight of that knife—"

"Hush!" came from many mouths.

"Oh, we want to forget it! Yes, we don't want to talk about it, I know. But I've got to this once. If there had been an accident—to Armitage—it wouldn't have been wholly the March Hare's fault. It was those who first started the quarrel between boarders and day-boys, those who put the notion of ill-feeling into his silly little head. I see you're thinking of the swimming-baths, and Toppin's dive. Now I happen to know, and Toppin can bear me out, that the kid asked to be pushed, and that Armitage would have saved him next moment if the March Hare hadn't jumped in and hindered things. And everyone of you who have listened and nodded to the March Hare's tale have added coal to the fire you might have quenched in a moment. And—and—and—and—" poor Jack was shaking and stammering with excitement, "what—what if it had—ended in—"

But there he sat down, leaving his sentence unfinished.

Cadbury was the first to reply, and that was not at once. Slowly he ruled a long, thick, black line in his exercise-book, then, pushing his chair away from the table, tilted it back, and spoke:

"Well, I don't know what anyone else thinks, but I'll tell you what I do. Brady's last sentence was certainly not fluent, and I shouldn't care to have to analyse it. As for the jokes in it, they were about as plentiful as wasps in January. All that's true enough. Still, nevertheless, speaking for my humble self, he thrust home. You did, Jack, you beggar! You'd no business to, but you actually had the impudence to make me feel ashamed of myself. And, of course, I don't know what you others will say, but I vote we bury the hatchet in old Thompson's biggest flower-pot. Who's with me?"

"I am!"

"I am!"

"And I!"

"Of course it's quite right to forgive," drawled Green, with a curl of the lip. "I'm more than willing."

Jack ground his teeth, but Hallett saved him the trouble of replying.

"No, no; if we do the thing at all, we'll do it properly. Don't let's have any half-measures—kindly-forgivings, and all the rest of it! If anyone starts forgiving me, I'll lick him! We won't forgive anyone, not even ourselves.

We'll go straight ahead on a new tack, and forget everything that's happened. If our friends the enemy look askance at us at first (and we needn't be surprised if they do), that mustn't affect us. Remember this: Scores are Settled. That's our motto; there is to be no more paying off. Chaff them if you like—I fancy they'd think there was something fishy if we didn't—but no tricks, if you please."

"What if they start them on us, Hallett?" enquired Grey, in the tone of one who merely seeks information. Hallett frowned slightly.

"Hadn't thought of that. Of course if they insist on picking a quarrel in that way—"

"But I'm nearly sure they won't," cried Jack.

"I caught Lucy pasting the leaves of my *Delectus* together," murmured Grey, looking at the ceiling.

"And how many things have you done to them?" retorted Jack desperately, sighing as he felt the weakness of that argument.

"Vick, will you hand Grey your india-rubber?" put in Cadbury. "There's a bit of his memory he hasn't rubbed out yet. I did as Hallett told us, and forgot everything at once. I've even forgotten my translation for to-morrow—it's gone entirely. Never mind: to obey is our first duty; to labour for Peace comes only second."

"Labouring for peace—why, Brady, that's been your little task!" exclaimed Vickers. "And a noble one"—here he put on the "West voice". "Have you thought of it in that light, my boy? To labour for peace! We might all do worse. Conceive, for instance, of working for love!"

Jack laughed noisily, and called Vickers "a silly old loony". But he blushed at the same time. And he went to sleep that night feeling uncommonly hopeful.

When, in short jerky phrases, he broke to Hannah the plan he had devised, the maid was so grateful and "took aback", as she said, as to become for the moment half-hysterical; but soon rallying her common sense, she sat down and penned a note to her father, to accompany the young gentlemen's communication. Hannah's spelling, handwriting, and grammar were all very shaky, but it is a fact that Mr. J. Thompson, Nurseryman, found her letter a help in throwing light upon the "formal, business" document.

CHAPTER IX. LOST — A NAME.

Of course Jack's task was only half accomplished. And the second half was somewhat harder than he had anticipated. When in the morning he met the day-scholars, they were not as eager for a reconciliation as he would have liked to find them.

Mason had come armed with a handful of wild barley-grass, or "crawly", as it was better known among the boys.

"*Dictée* this morning," he said with a sly wink.

In Monsieur Blonde's class, dictation offered great possibilities to a quick writer, with a supply of crawly. When heads are bent, what a chance down the collar for a deft hand! And the Monsieur was very short-sighted.

"I sit between Vickers and Green," Mason added.

"But look here, you must chuck that stuff away," cried Jack. He knew that as a good-humoured joke an inch of crawly can be tolerated, but when used in malice, nothing is more irritating. "Chuck it away! We've all agreed to call *Pax* now, *Pax* for good and all."

"Oh, I dare say!" retorted Mason. "When our lives have been made a burden for the last week! Who are the 'all' who've agreed, pray?"

"The whole lot of the boarders. They're ready to chum up right away. Mason, you must agree! We've got to join forces over Saturday's job."

But Mason didn't see it. Nor did Armitage. Nor did Bacon. And the rest were doubtful, except little Frere, who declared at once that he was longing to be friends with everybody — and to feel safe.

"But don't mind us, Brady," pursued Mason. "We aren't so sweet on shoving wheel-barrows as all that. You and your dear Green and the rest can have the whole glory and honour of the pots and the barrows to yourselves. We won't fight for them, will we? After all, there are more amusing ways of spending a half than in wheeling flower-pots round the town."

Jack's hopes sank. He did not feel equal to making a second speech, but he caught Mason by the arm, and spoke with vehement emphasis:

"It's an awful responsible thing, Mason, to refuse to patch a quarrel. The chance of making-up doesn't come every day."

"We must have a chance of getting even with them first, and then we'll talk about stopping."

"Nonsense! You know that tit-for-tat's a game without an end!"

"My dear Brady, if you knew the toil and time it has cost me to gather this bunch of crawly, you wouldn't ask me so lightly to waste it."

"If that's all," said Jack, "you can stick the whole lot down my neck. I give you free leave. Go on!"

There is no stronger influence than earnestness, and Jack was intensely in earnest. It had its effect on his listeners, who were almost won over already, while he thought his efforts were thrown away. While he spoke, Simmons had secretly released three earwigs with which he had meant mischief, and Hughes was opening his mouth to utter a word or two for Jack, when Cadbury glided up to the group with outspread arms, and a square box balanced on his head.

"Pax tea-cup! pax O biscuit!" began the flippant boy. "Dear brethren, I entreat you to join with me in smoking the calumet of peace in the shape of this humble weed."

As he bowed, the box fell from his head into his hands, and, removing the lid, he offered it round. It appeared to contain a double layer of cigars; but the Brincliffe scholars knew these cigars well, and where they came from. They were composed of almond paste, and coated with a brown sugary paper, which was always consumed with the rest.

Jack almost held his breath. Would the boys refuse or accept them?

Hughes dipped his hand in at once with a smile and a nod. "Thanks very much, Cadbury!" Simmons followed suit with a wicked little chuckle.

Bacon hesitated, and then helped himself awkwardly. Frere took one with an "Oo!" of appreciation. Now it was Mason's turn. If Jack had been a recruiting sergeant, and the sugar cigar the Queen's shilling, he could scarcely have felt more anxious.

Mason put forward his thumb and finger, then hesitated and looked at Jack with a twinkle in his eye.

"Now, shall I, Brady?"

Jack nodded. He really dared not speak, for fear Mason should take it into his head to go exactly contrary to him.

Hurrah! The cigar was taken!

From that moment Cadbury and Jack turned themselves into a couple of the maddest, silliest clowns imaginable. But there was method in their madness. Though they did not even own it to each other, they were making themselves ridiculous and foolish to prevent the rest from feeling so. Boys loathe sentiment, and many a quarrel drifts on and on, simply because each party dreads "being made to feel a fool".

At Brincliffe on this particular day the two sides felt distinctly shy of each other, and it was a real boon to have a pair of "giddy lunatics" to scream at.

But when Cadbury had boxed Frere's ears for giving the dates of the royal Georges correctly, and when Simmons had sharpened his pencil with Vickers's knife without asking leave, the relations between boarders and day-pupils grew easier.

There were few idle wheel-barrows in Elmridge on Saturday afternoon.

If you had passed along the dusty Brickland Road between four and five o'clock, you would have encountered a droll procession. One passer-by stopped to enquire if there was going to be a Battle of Flowers.

Six barrows, laden with flowering plants, each pulled by two boys, and pushed by one, were slowly but steadily travelling towards the town, and at the rear of all was a bath-chair in charge of Hallett and Armitage, wherein sat a thin, delicate-looking man, whose bright eyes and flushed cheeks spoke eloquently of gratitude and pleasure. That bath-chair was Hallett's own idea, and he was very proud of it.

It was a warm and weary company of boy-labourers who gathered at eight o'clock that evening round a very tempting supper-table, spread in the Brincliffe dining-room, to which, by special invitation, the day-pupils sat down with the boarders. But every face was bright, and the meal was the merriest ever known.

By Mr. West's direction, the boys were left to enjoy it "un-mastered".

The clatter of knives and spoons had almost ceased when Vickers rose slowly to his feet, a glass of ginger-beer in his hand. He was impelled to do so by the nudges of his neighbours, Green and Mason. His rising was received with loud applause, which he acknowledged with a grave bow.

"I have been very much pressed—elbow-pressed," he began, "to get up and say something. I scarcely see why I should be pitched on, unless it is because I have more brass than the rest of you. (Hear, hear.) Anyhow, here I am, and I'll ask three questions and then sit down. First"—and up came one finger—"Isn't this the jolliest supper we've ever had? (Cries of "Yes!") Very well, I'll tell you why. Reason Number One: West's in a jolly good temper, *vide* the groaning table and the absence of masters. Reason Number Two: We're all in a jolly good temper, and have done a jolly good day's work. Now, secondly—(Shouts of "Thirdly, you mean, old man!") I mean what I say—Secondly! We had two divisions under the first head. You may have got confused, but I haven't. Secondly, then, we're all pretty thoroughly fagged: is anyone sorry he's fagged? (No!) Well, the job wasn't my idea, or West's idea. But it was somebody's, and I think we all know whose. The same somebody who has annoyed us all horribly in the past by refusing to so much as do one ill-natured thing. The same somebody who has steadily prevented us from quarrelling comfortably and consistently, as we wanted to, and has finally dragged us into this unhappy state of good-fellowship. Now for my thirdly: Will you drink with me to that somebody's health?"

The question was received with shouting and banging, while the words, "Bravo, Vickers! Here's to good old Brady!" "I drink to Jack of Both Sides!" "Here's to you, Jack!" "Speech, Brady—speech!" and similar cries filled the air.

Poor Jack felt extremely ill at ease, and not at all grateful to Vickers. He studied his plate with the closest attention, his face growing redder and redder each moment. Then Cadbury thumped him on the back, and Hallett and Bacon fairly forced him to his feet. But a speech was quite beyond Jack at that minute.

"I say, sha'n't we beg the release of the March Hare?" was all he said, and the first person he looked at was Armitage.

Armitage, too, was the first to cry back, "Yes!"

The petition, which was written and signed before they separated, was received favourably, and the following Monday saw the return of the March Hare to his place in the school, scared, penitent, and profoundly grateful to all his school-fellows, including Armitage. And he insisted on pressing Jack's hand to his lips, which made our hero feel excessively uncomfortable. But for the remainder of the term, the use of a knife, even at dinner, was denied the little Italian.

"Brady, have you missed anything?" asked Cadbury a few days later.

"No, I don't think so," replied Jack, feeling doubtfully in his pockets.

"Because you have certainly lost something," continued Cadbury.

"Well, give it me quick, then," said Jack, laughing. "Whatever is it?"

"I can't give it you. It's gone for ever," was the rejoinder. "You'll never have it again."

"Well, what was it, then? Nothing valuable, I hope?"

"When two things are made into one thing, you can't speak of them any longer as 'both'; can you?"

"Fetch us a grammar, Toppin," said Jack. "We're getting out of our depths. Have I lost two things, please, Cadbury, or only one?"

"Don't frivol, Jack! listen to me. We are all one-sided now, so you have lost your title. You can never again be called Jack of Both Sides."